Ann Schweninger

Halloween Surprises

·BUTTON BROWN· ·MOTHER· ·BUTTERCUP· ·DAISY· ·FATHER·

Puffin Books

For Deborah Brodie and Barbara Hennessy

PUFFIN BOOKS
A Division of Penguin Books USA Inc.
375 Hudson Street, New York, New York 10014
Penguin Books Ltd, Harmondsworth, Middlesex, England
Penguin Books Australia Ltd, Ringwood, Victoria, Australia
Penguin Books Canada Limited, 2801 John Street, Markham, Ontario, Canada L3R 1B4
Penguin Books (N.Z.) Ltd, 182–190 Wairau Road, Auckland 10, New Zealand

First published by Viking Penguin Inc. 1984
Published in Picture Puffins 1986
Reprinted 1991
Copyright © Ann Schweninger, 1984
All rights reserved
Printed in Japan by Dai Nippon Printing Co. Ltd.
Set in Windsor

Library of Congress Cataloging in Publication Data
Schweninger, Ann.   Halloween surprises.
Summary: After the Rabbit children have celebrated Halloween by
making costumes, carving jack-o-lanterns, and going trick-or-treating,
their parents have one more surprise in store for them.
[1. Halloween—Fiction.   2. Rabbits—Fiction]   I. Title.
PZ7.S41263Hal 1986   [E]   86-3275   ISBN 0-14-050634-9

Costumes

YOU COULD BE A DEVIL.
OR A SKELETON.
I'LL BE A SCARECROW.
I'LL BE A MONSTER.

DAISY, WHAT ARE YOU GOING TO BE?

Jack-O-Lanterns

VERY SCARY!

Trick or Treat